Dear Parent:
Your child's love of reading starts here!

Every child learns to read in a different way and at his or her own speed. Some go back and forth between reading levels and read favorite books again and again. Others read through each level in order. You can help your young reader improve and become more confident by encouraging his or her own interests and abilities. From books your child reads with you to the first books he or she reads alone, there are I Can Read Books for every stage of reading:

SHARED READING
Basic language, word repetition, and whimsical illustrations, ideal for sharing with your emergent reader

BEGINNING READING
Short sentences, familiar words, and simple concepts for children eager to read on their own

READING WITH HELP
Engaging stories, longer sentences, and language play for developing readers

READING ALONE
Complex plots, challenging vocabulary, and high-interest topics for the independent reader

ADVANCED READING
Short paragraphs, chapters, and exciting themes for the perfect bridge to chapter books

I Can Read Books have introduced children to the joy of reading since 1957. Featuring award-winning authors and illustrators and a fabulous cast of beloved characters, I Can Read Books set the standard for beginning readers.

A lifetime of discovery begins with the magical words "I Can Read!"

Visit www.icanread.com for information
on enriching your child's reading experience.

I Can Read Book® is a trademark of HarperCollins Publishers.

Flat Stanley: On Ice
Text copyright © 2015 by the Trust u/w/o Richard C. Brown a/k/a Jeff Brown f/b/o Duncan Brown.
Illustrations by Macky Pamintuan, copyright © 2015 by HarperCollins Publishers.
All rights reserved. Manufactured in China. No part of this book may be used or reproduced in any manner whatsoever without
written permission except in the case of brief quotations embodied in critical articles and reviews. For information address
HarperCollins Children's Books, a division of HarperCollins Publishers, 195 Broadway, New York, NY 10007.
www.icanread.com
Library of Congress catalog card number: 2014958869
ISBN 978-0-06-218982-0 (trade bdg.)—ISBN 978-0-06-218981-3 (pbk.)
Typography by Jeff Shake

15 16 17 18 19   SCP   10 9 8 7 6 5 4 3 2 1   ❖   First Edition

I Can Read!

READING 2 WITH HELP

FLAT STANLEY

On Ice

created by Jeff Brown
by Lori Haskins Houran
pictures by Macky Pamintuan

HARPER

An Imprint of HarperCollinsPublishers

Stanley Lambchop lived

with his mother,

his father,

and his little brother, Arthur.

Stanley was four feet tall,

about a foot wide,

and half an inch thick.

He had been flat ever since

a bulletin board fell on him.

Stanley was still discovering

new things about being flat.

It turned out he was great

at catching snowflakes!

Stanley was not so great

at making snow angels.

"You're too flat to sink into the snow!"

said Arthur.

"Never mind," said Stanley.

"Let's just head to the skating pond."

They saw lots of people

they knew out skating.

"Hi, Arthur! Hi, Stanley!"
called their friend Martin Tibbs.
Coach Bart waved hello.
"I can't wait to get on the ice!"
said Arthur, grabbing his skates.

Now that Stanley's feet were flat, they didn't fit into skates anymore. But Stanley wondered if he could just use his feet as skates!

"I hope this works," he said.

Stanley stood up on the ice.

He pushed off with his left foot,

then his right.

WHOOSH!

He took off!

Stanley couldn't believe
how terrific he was at skating.
It was his best flat discovery yet!

"Look at him spin!" said Martin.

"Did he just carve his name in the ice?" asked Coach Bart.

"I can make a snow angel," said Arthur.

Stanley swooped and glided
for hours.
Arthur skated, too,
though he did more sliding
than gliding.

"Phew! I'm hot,"

said Arthur after a while.

He took off his jacket.

"Me, too," said Martin.

They weren't the only ones

who felt it getting warmer.

15

Coach Bart blew his whistle.

"Everyone off the ice!"

"Noooo!" complained the skaters.

"I brought hot chocolate!" he said.

In six seconds, the ice was empty.

Except for Stanley, still skating
in the middle of the pond.

"STAN-LEY!" yelled Arthur.

"STAN-LEY!" yelled Martin.

Out on the ice, Stanley heard his name.
"Wow," he said. "They're cheering!
I'd better put on a good show."

Stanley got going fast.

He pushed hard off his big toe

and did a split in the air!

When he landed, there was a loud POP.

Stanley looked down.

The ice was cracking—

right between his feet!

"Help!" cried Stanley. "HELP!"

Arthur shouted back at him.

"LIE DOWN, STANLEY!

MAKE A SNOW ANGEL!"

"Sheesh," thought Stanley.

Was this really the time to tease him

about snow angels?

 So what if he was too flat

to sink into the snow . . .

Then Stanley understood.

If he lay down on the ice,

he would be too flat to sink!

Carefully, Stanley spread out.

He was safe for now.

But how would he get off the ice?

Back on shore, Arthur was busy.

"We need a rope!" he called.

"Help me tie the scarves together.

The arms of the jackets, too!"

"Good thinking, Arthur,"

said Coach Bart.

"We're on it!" said Martin.

All the skaters pitched in.

Soon they had a long rope

to toss to Stanley.

Stanley caught it on the first try.

"PULL!" ordered Arthur.

Everyone gave a mighty tug.

Stanley came flying across the ice!

Stanley flew a little *too* well—
off the ice, past the skaters,
and straight into a snow bank!

"I'm okay!" said Stanley,

spitting out a mouthful of snow.

Coach Bart poured hot chocolate
for everyone.

He raised his mug.

"Here's to Arthur Lambchop,
who kept his cool
when things got warm!"

"Yay, Arthur!" everyone cheered.

Stanley cheered loudest of all.

And the next time the pond froze,

Stanley gave Arthur an extra-big thanks.